MAZIE'S
AMAZING
MACHINES

LIBRARY LIFTER

Nancy Paulsen Books

WITHDRAWN

MAZIE-VATOR

written by SHERYL HAFT   illustrated by JEREMY HOLMES

My name is Mazie McGear. What I love to do is *engineer*! I'm the small one in my family, but I always wear a *big* belt full of tools. My favorite is the crank drill.

Engineers like to make up inventions to fix *problems*. Like how I have to feed my dog, Doodle, so early every morning.

That's a **PROBLEM**.

First, I turn on my imagination . . .

THINK

BLINK

Then I draw . . .

RIBBLE

SCRIBBLE

Then . . .
I build!

BING BANG BOOM

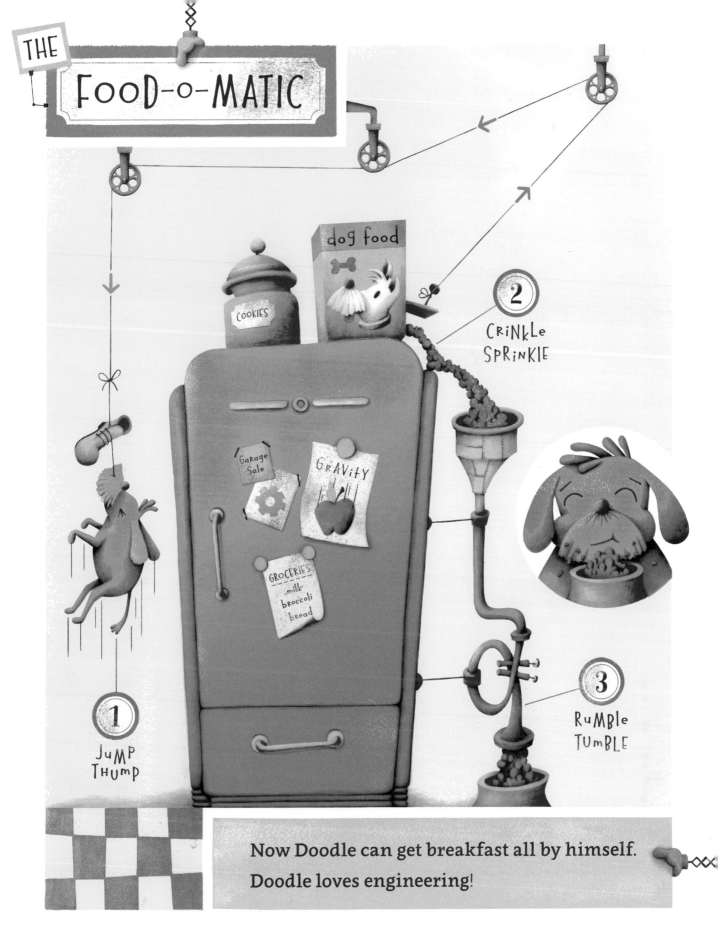

THE
FOOD-O-MATIC

COOKIES

dog food

Garage Sale

GRAVITY

GROCERIES
milk
broccoli
bread

1 JUMP THUMP

2 CRINKLE SPRINKLE

3 RUMBLE TUMBLE

Now Doodle can get breakfast all by himself. Doodle loves engineering!

I find more problems around my house. It's hard for Mom to carry a stack of heavy boxes.

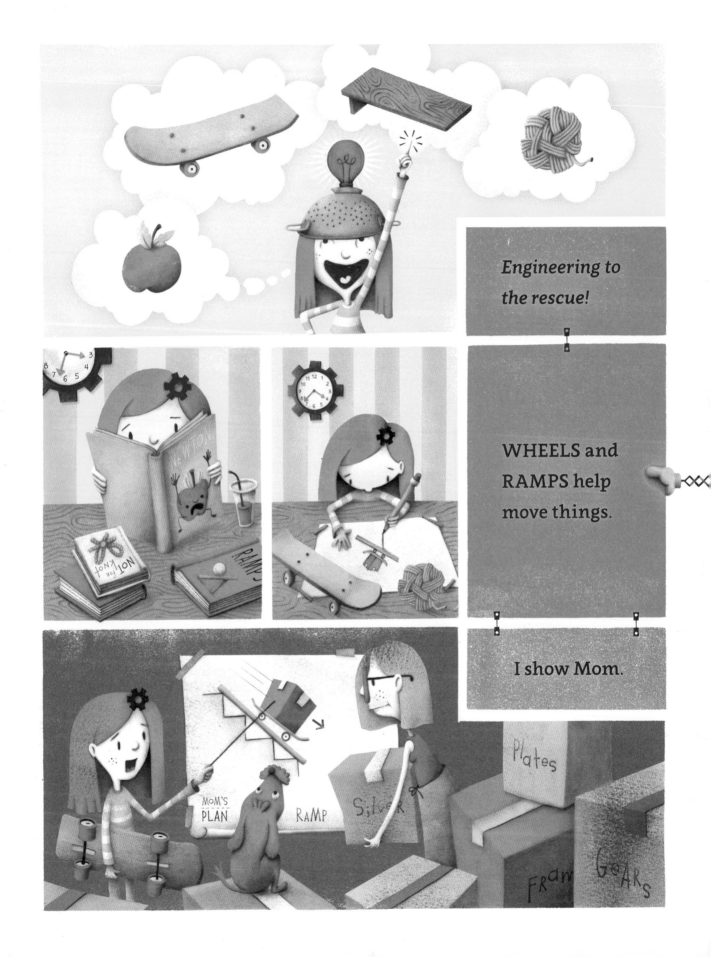

Engineering to
the rescue!

WHEELS and
RAMPS help
move things.

I show Mom.

I MAKE A

ROLY-
RAMP

1 PUSH

2 WHOOSH

Mom's happy, but when I bump into my big brother, Jake, he is NOT.

Ahhh! Engineering is an *engi-nuisance!*

Now Dad needs help lifting a tire up onto the garage shelf.

I BUILD HIM A

PULLEY-LIFTER!

Jake has a **PROBLEM** too.
He can *never* wake up in the morning.

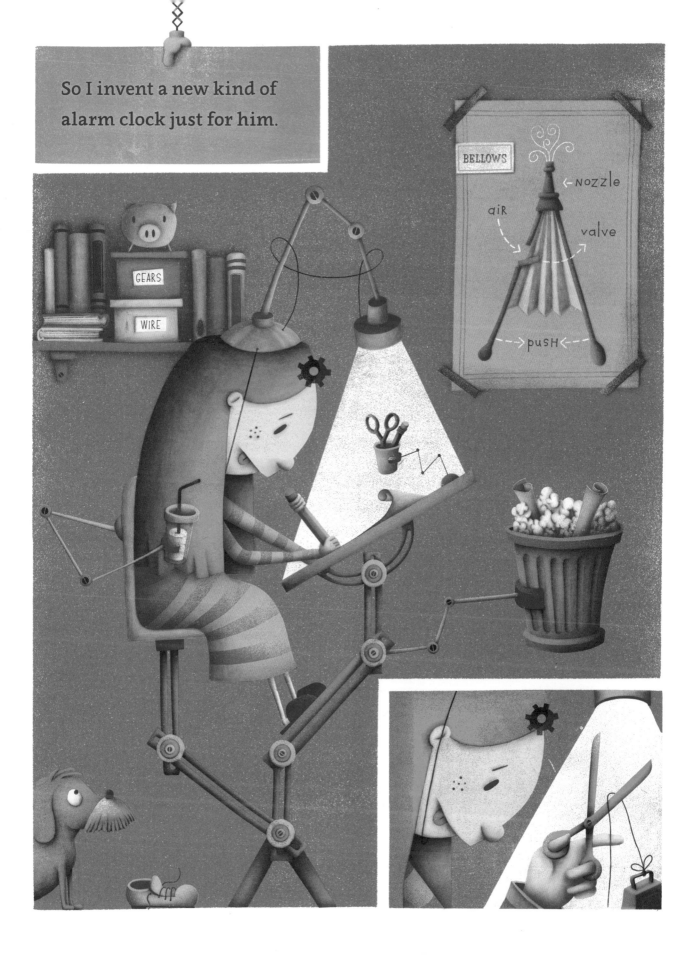

So I invent a new kind of alarm clock just for him.

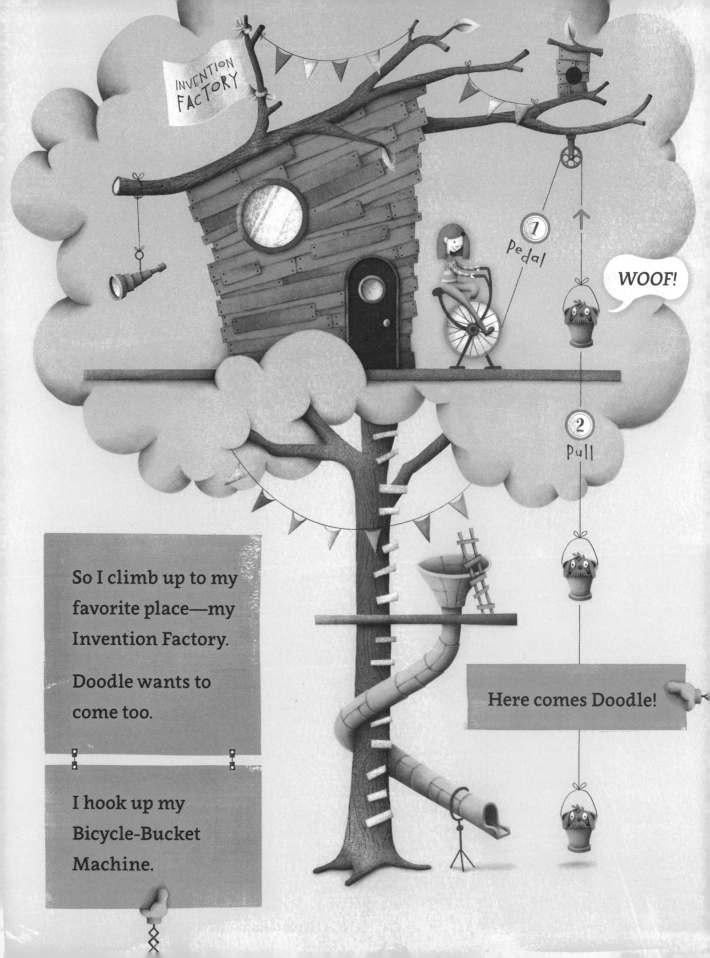

So I climb up to my favorite place—my Invention Factory.

Doodle wants to come too.

I hook up my Bicycle-Bucket Machine.

That's when I see Jake throwing a basketball. He can't get the ball into the net.

That's a . . .
PROBLEM.
Maybe I can help.

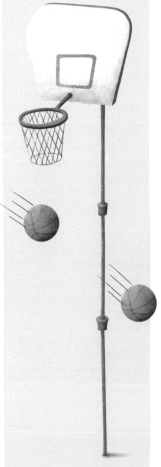

THINK

BLINK

I imagine.

I draw.

RIBBLE

SCRIBBLE

CRANK

I build.

I'm going to WOW Jake with an invention that's *amazing!*

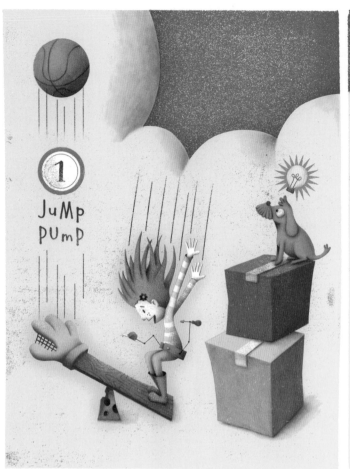

Now I climb up
extra high.

Help!

Mom and Dad come running.
We try a ladder.
We can't reach Doodle.

Doodle starts to cry.

I cry.

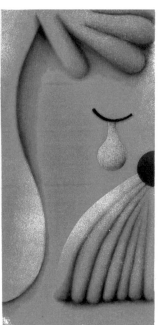

This is a *BIG* problem!

THINK BLINK

My family imagines lots and lots of ideas.

That's called a *brainstorm*!

RIBBLE SCRIBBLE

We draw and draw.

Then we get a *Big Idea*.

Mom gets the
Roly-Ramp.

Dad grabs the
Pulley-Lifter.

Jake brings the
Teeter-Lever.

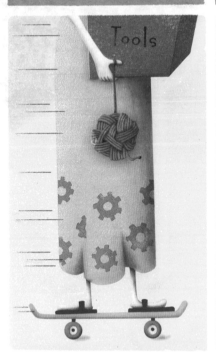

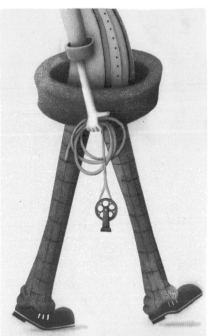

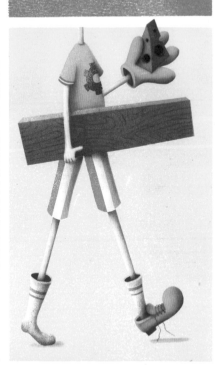

Wow!
My whole family is
engineering!

We connect all of the little
machines into one big
Kinetic Contraption.

THE PULLEY–POWER–SAVE–OUR–DOG TOWER

(1)

THUMP
stomps Jake.

My family loops
into a group hug.
We fit together
like the parts of a
whole new kind of
invention . . .

A

HUG-A-LOVE
MACHINE

And it's
amazing.

SNUGGLE WUGGLE

Mazie's 6 Simple Machines

Engineers use **SIMPLE MACHINES** to make it easier to lift or move things:

PULLEY: A grooved wheel with a rope around it. A pulley helps move a load up or down.

WHEEL & AXLE: A wheel with a rod, called an axle, through its center makes it easier to push or move things.

LEVER: A bar that pivots on a support called a fulcrum. A lever reduces the effort needed to lift or move a load.

INCLINED PLANE: A slanted surface. An inclined plane makes it easier to move a load up or down.

WEDGE: Two inclined planes forming a thin edge. A wedge increases force to help secure or split materials.

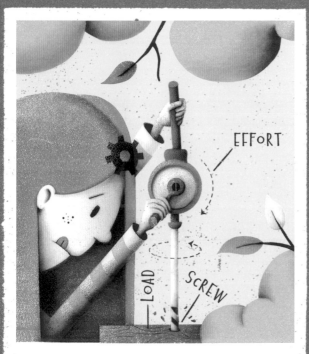

SCREW: An inclined plane wrapped in a spiral. A screw helps move a load or hold things together.

What problems would you like to solve? What inventions can you imagine? **Let's engineer!**

WOOF!

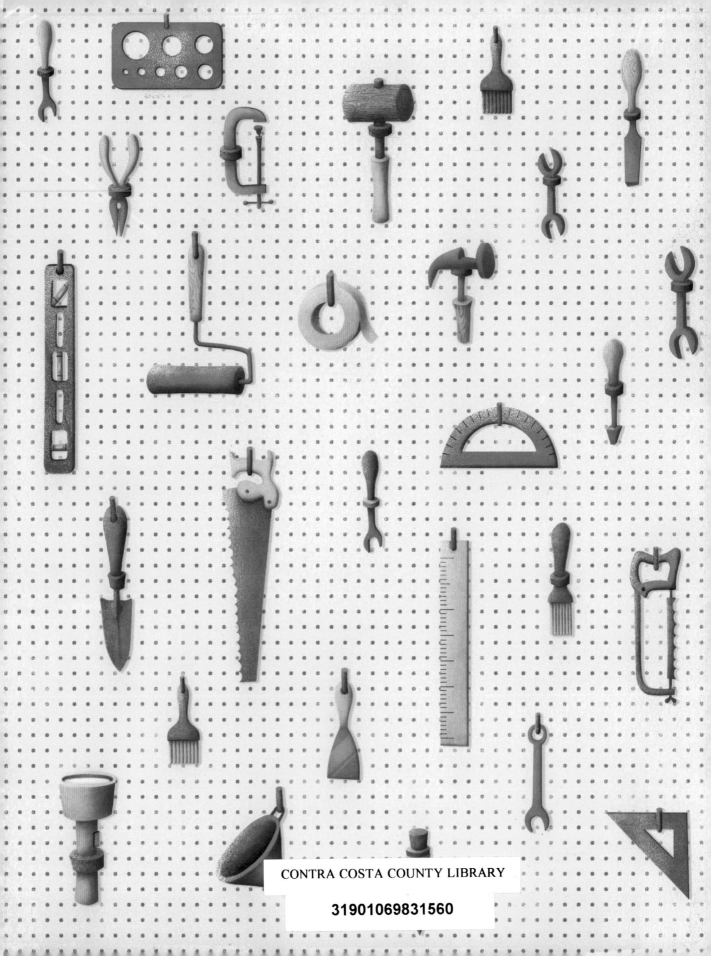